Peppa Pig World

Souvenir Storybook

Oink!

I'm Peppa. I hope you enjoy whizzing around on all the fun rides at Peppa Pig World – and jumping up and down in all the muddy puddles!

If you need to find your way around, this book has a brilliant map inside that shows you where everything is. Remember to come and see us all in our house, where Mummy Pig is teaching George and me how to make pancakes. I love pancakes – they are yummy!

There are lots of stories and games and puzzles, too. You can read them when you get home, to remind you of all the fun you had at Peppa Pig World.

Peppa x x

Muddy Puddles

Miss Rabbit's Helicopter Flight

Peppa Pig's House

Daddy Pig's Car Ride

Pedro Pony's Photo Kiosk

George's Dinosaur Adventure

Mr. Potato's Playground

Windy Castle

Peppa's Big Balloon Ride

Grandpa Pig's Little Train

Miss Rabbit's Ice Cream Parlour

Madame Gazelle's School House

see Peppa and George here!

Daddy Pig's Big Tummy Cafe

Candy Cat's Games Kiosk

The Queen's flying Coach Ride

Peppa Pig's Toy Shop

Grandpa Pig's Boat Trip

George's Spaceship Play Zone

Grampy Rabbit's Sailing Club

Peppa Pig World

My Big Day Out

Draw yourself next to Peppa and George on your favourite ride at Peppa Pig World!

Me, Peppa and George on the

....

Things I did at Peppa Pig World . . .

I went on:

I ate:

I saw:

I met:

Bus Trip

Madame Gazelle is taking Peppa and her friends on a day trip on the bus. What can they see out of the window?

Where do you think Peppa and her friends are going?

Tick the boxes for everything you can see in the big picture.

Dinosaur

Sun

Tree

House

Mountain

Cloud

Duck

Car

Ball

Teddy

Madame Gazelle's "Bing Bong" Song

We're playing a tune
and we're singing a song,
with a bing and a bong,
and a bing!

Bong-bing-boo,
Bing-bong-bing,
Bing-bong,
Bingly-bungly-boo!

Bong-bing-boo,
Bing-bong-bing,
Bing-bong,
Bingly-bungly-boo!

Pretend you're on a bus, too, and sing along with Madame Gazelle, Peppa and her friends!

Bong-bing-boo,
Bing-bong-bing,
Bing-bong,
Bingly-bungly-boo!

Peppa's Big Day Out

Join Peppa and her friends on their
brilliant adventure at Potato City!

Peppa is visiting a
theme park called
Potato City.
"Two adults and two
children, please," says Mummy Pig.
Miss Rabbit prints out the tickets. "There's so much
to do in Potato City," she says. "Have a lovely day!"

Peppa's friends have
come to visit, too.
Suzy Sheep is pretending
to be a tomato.
"Busy, isn't it?" gulps Daddy Pig.
"It's fantastic!" says Peppa.

Just then, everybody gasps – Mr Potato has arrived! "Welcome to Potato City," he cries. "Where the magic of vegetables never ends!" "Hooray!" cheer Peppa and her friends.

Mr Potato takes the children to the dinosaur garden.
Suzy is confused. "Why have you got dinosaurs in Potato City?"
"Erm . . ." Mr Potato frowns, "because dinosaurs like eating potatoes?"
Suzy shakes her head. It's because children like dinosaurs!

"Roll up, roll up for the Vegetable-Roundabout-Swing-Thing!" calls Mr Potato. Everybody loves the Vegetable-Roundabout-Swing-Thing! Peppa and her friends jump on and ride it again and again . . . and again.

"I like Potato City because it teaches you about vegetables," cries Peppa, "and swings you round and round!" But there is still one ride that Peppa hasn't been on yet – the Potato Rocket!

Peppa and her friends climb into the carriages.
George wants to go on, too. Daddy Pig isn't sure.
The Potato Rocket looks very high.
"Oh, OK," Daddy Pig snorts. "Make it quick."

Aaaaaahhhhhhhhhh!

George changes his mind
and gets off. But it is too
late for Daddy Pig.
"I love the Potato Rocket!"
shouts Suzy.
"I love Potato City!"
shouts Peppa.
"HOORAAAAAY!"
everyone shouts together.

Rollercoaster Ride!

Join the dots to finish the rollercoaster carriages and take Peppa, Emily, Suzy and Daddy Pig for the ride of a lifetime! Draw yourself in the empty carriage.

Dino Adventure!

At Potato City, George is riding the triceratops and Richard is on the stegosaurus. But where will they end up? Follow or draw over the dotted lines to find out!

Dinosaur Spotting!

George and Peppa are in the forest, looking for dinosaurs. Can you see any?

Draw a tick or colour in the box next to each dinosaur when you find it.

Peppa Goes Camping

Honk! Honk! Peppa and her family are going on holiday in a very special camper van . . .

"We're going on holiday!" sings Peppa. "We're going on holiday, in our camper van."

"Hmmm," says Daddy Pig, looking at the map.

"Daddy Pig!" cries Mummy Pig. "Are we lost?"

"Well, er . . ." begins Daddy Pig. "Yes."

Grandad Dog and Danny Dog arrive.

"Hello," calls out Peppa. "We're lost!"

"Is your sat nav broken?" asks Grandad Dog. Mummy and Daddy Pig don't know what a sat nav is.

"A sat nav is a computer that helps you find your way," explains Grandad Dog.
"Can you tell us where to go?" Peppa asks the sat nav.
"Go straight," replies the sat nav.
Daddy Pig thanks Grandad Dog, and the family continue on their way.
Suddenly, the camper van is low on oil, but Daddy Pig can't find the engine!
Mummy Sheep and Suzy Sheep arrive.
"Hello, Suzy," cries Peppa. "We've lost our engine."
"I don't know a thing about engines," says Mummy Sheep.
"But I'll have a look."

"This looks like an engine," says Mummy Sheep, lifting the boot.
"Well spotted," says Daddy Pig, pouring oil into the engine. Glug! Glug!
Daddy Pig thanks Mummy Sheep and the family set off again.

"Are we nearly there yet?"
asks Peppa, sighing.
"You have reached your
destination," announces
the sat nav.
"Hooray!" everyone cheers.

"Where will we sleep?" asks Peppa.

"Mummy Pig and I will sleep on this bed," says Daddy Pig, pressing a button. Whirr! A lovely big bed appears.
"And watch this," says Daddy Pig, pressing another button . . .

Suddenly, the camper van's roof lifts up and a bunk bed appears! Daddy Pig tucks Peppa and George into bed.
"The camper van is just like our little house!" says Peppa.
"Goodnight, everyone," says the sat nav. "Sleep well!"

Daddy Pig's Car Wash

Daddy Pig loves his camper van, but he loves his car, too! Help Peppa and George clean their car by using the numbers to colour in the picture.

Colour key

1 2
3 4
5 6

1

4   4   4   4

4

2

1   1

1

2

2

1

1   1

6   6
6
6

5   5

1

5   5   5

7

7

5
5
5

Grandpa's Train Trouble

Oh dear! Grandpa Pig's train has broken. Help him put it back together again. All you need to do is draw a circle around the BIGGEST thing in each row.

1.   a   b   c   d   e   f   g   h   i

2.   a   b   c   d   e

3.   a   b   c   d   e   f   g   h   i

Thank you
for your help!

Grampy Rabbit's Sailing Club

Ahoy there! Grampy Rabbit is teaching everyone how to sail by singing a song! Trace the numbers to count how many of each thing Peppa and George can spot out at sea.

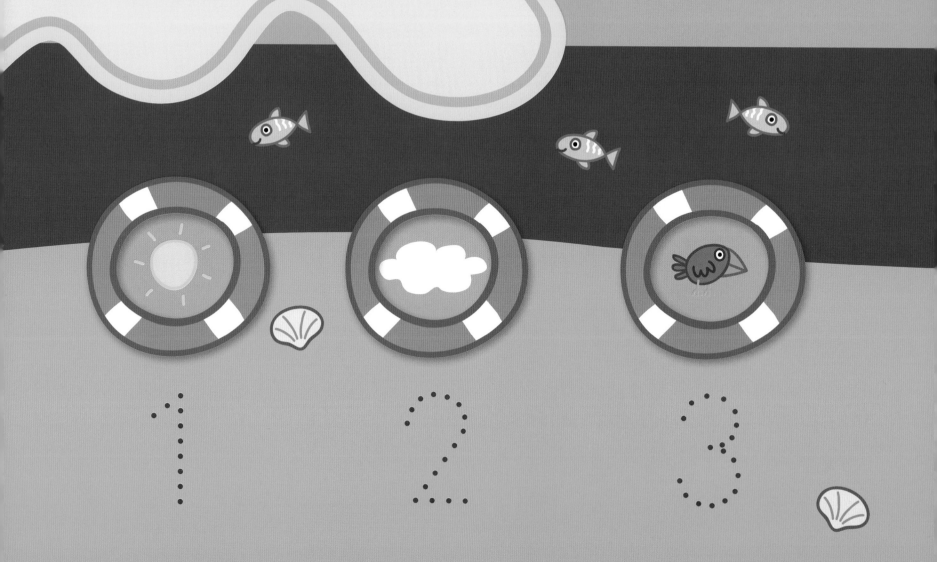

George's Balloon

George loves his dinosaur balloon, but who will rescue it when it starts floating all the way to the moon?

Granny and Grandpa Pig are at Miss Rabbit's ice cream stall.
"I think George wants a dinosaur balloon, not an ice cream," says Miss Rabbit.
"All right, how much is it?" Grandpa Pig asks.
"Ten pounds, please," says Miss Rabbit.

Grandpa Pig buys the balloon for George.
"Hold on tight to it," Miss Rabbit says.
But George lets go and the balloon starts to float away.
Grandpa quickly grabs the string,
"This is very valuable, George.
I'll hold it on the way home."

George plays with his balloon outside Granny and Grandpa Pig's house.
"It's an up balloon, George," says Peppa. "If you let it go, it will go up
to the moon!"
"Moon!" George says, letting the balloon go.
Grandpa Pig catches it just before it zooms off.

Peppa and George go inside to
keep the balloon safe.
"Hello, Polly," says Peppa.
"George has got a new balloon!"
"Squawk!" cries Polly Parrot.
"Balloon."
Polly loves George's balloon.

George lets go of the balloon. The balloon floats all the way out the door, up the stairs into the attic . . . and escapes out of the open attic window!

"Oh no!" cries George. "Your balloon is going to the moon, George!" says Peppa.

Just then, Daddy Pig arrives to take Peppa and George home. "Oh dear," says Daddy Pig, seeing George crying. "There must be some way we can get the balloon back," says Granny Pig. "Squawk! Balloon!" says Polly.

Polly flies high up into the sky and catches the balloon string in her beak. "Polly to the rescue!" cries Grandpa Pig. Polly Parrot has saved the day. "Hooray!" cheers George.

Daddy Pig ties the balloon string to George's wrist.
"That will stop it floating away."
George is very happy. He loves his balloon.
Everyone loves George's balloon!

Snort!

Snort!

Balloon Shadows

It's the perfect day for a hot-air balloon ride! Peppa and George are matching balloons in the air with shadows on the ground. Draw lines between each balloon and its shadow to help.

Secret Island!

Grandpa Pig has taken Peppa and George out on his boat and they've discovered a secret island! Who do you think lives there? Draw something to surprise Peppa and George.

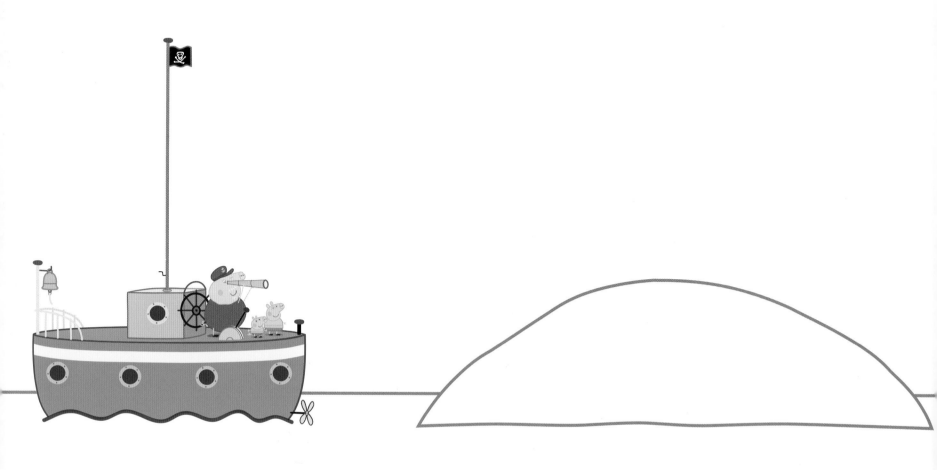

Missing Pieces!

Miss Rabbit is taking Peppa and George for a ride in her helicopter! But what's missing?
Draw lines to connect the parts to their correct places before Miss Rabbit takes off!

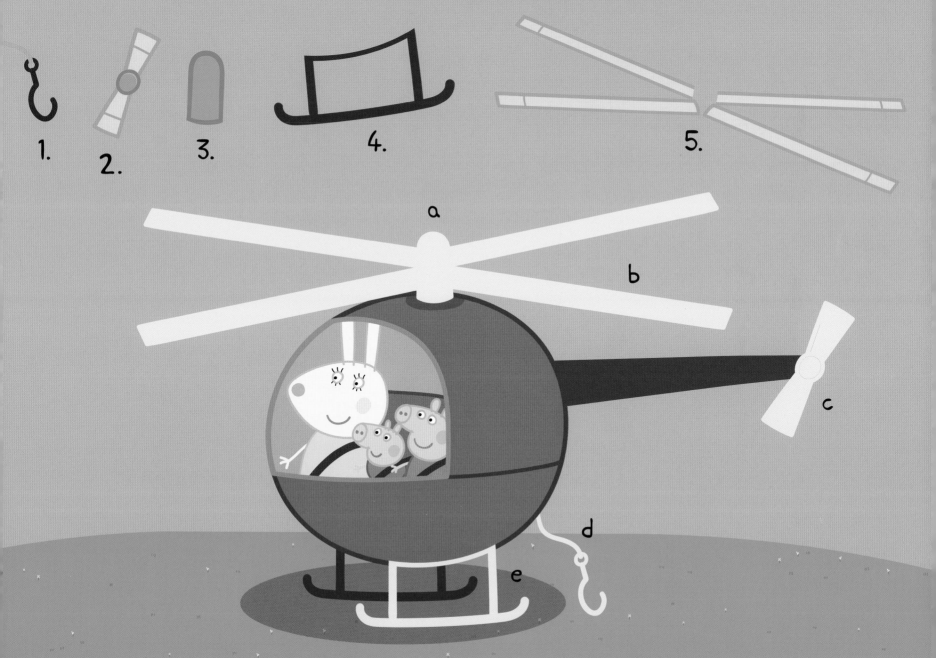

1.

2.

3.

4.

5.

a

b

c

d

e

Fun at the Fair

Roll up! Roll up! Peppa, George and their family are going for a day out to the funfair!

Peppa and her family are at the funfair.
"Slidey! Slidey!" giggles George.
"George wants to go on the helter-skelter," says Daddy Pig. So George and Daddy Pig head off to the helter-skelter.

"Roll up! Roll up!" cries Miss Rabbit. "Hook a duck and win a giant teddy!"

"I'll try to win one for you, Peppa," says Mummy Pig.
"It's impossible!" laughs Miss Rabbit.
"We'll see about that!" cries Mummy Pig.

Sploosh! Mummy Pig has hooked a duck!
"Hooray!" cheers Peppa.
"That's amazing!" cries Miss Rabbit.
"Here's your giant teddy!"

George and Daddy Pig are sliding down the helter-skelter.
"Hee! Hee! Wheeeeee!" cheers George.
"Wooahhh!" cries Daddy Pig. It is a bit too high for Daddy Pig.

Peppa and Mummy Pig are at the "hit the target" stall.
"Ho! Ho! You won't win!" laughs Mr Labrador.
"What did you say?" says Mummy Pig crossly.
She picks up the bow and arrow, and aims . . .

Whoosh! The arrow hits
the target right in the
middle. Mummy Pig
wins again!
"Unbelievable," cries
Mr Labrador. "Here's
your teddy!"
"Hooray!" cheers Peppa.

Daddy Pig and George find Peppa and Mummy Pig at the "hit the button with a hammer" stall. Mummy Pig picks up the hammer and hits the button as hard as she can. Whack!
The bell rings loudly. Ding! Ding!

Everyone is very impressed. Mummy Pig wins all the giant teddies at the fair!

"Hooray!" cheers Peppa, giving her friends a giant teddy each.
"Hooray!" everyone cheers. "We love funfairs!"

All the Rides!

Peppa and her family want to visit every ride and stall at the funfair! Follow the numbers and draw the path they should take from start to finish.

4

1
START

2

How many giant teddy bears did you see on the way?

. . . .

5

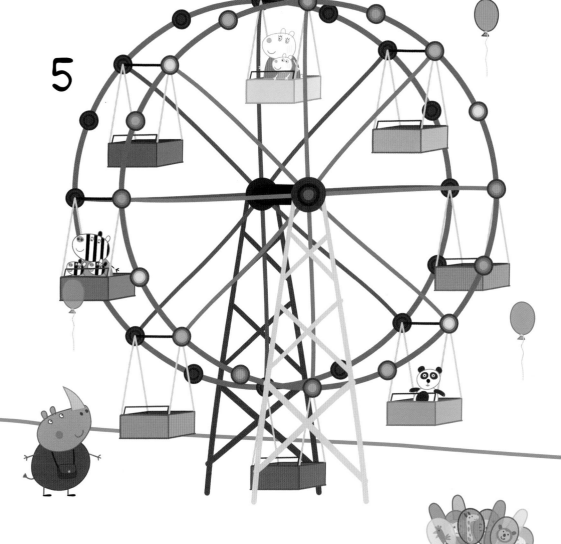

3

Don't forget to stop for an ice cream break at the finish!

6

FINISH

Answer: There are 7 giant teddies.

Stop!

Daddy Pig is stuck at a red light while Mr Bull and his team repair the road. Find your colouring pens or pencils and use the little picture to help you colour in the big one before the light turns green.

Matching Vehicles

Drill, drill, dig, dig! Mr Bull is mending the road. Can you draw lines to put all his construction vehicles into matching pairs? Which one is the odd one out?

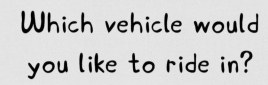
Which vehicle would you like to ride in?

Answer: Peppa's car is the odd one out.

Sleepy Princess

It's bedtime. What Peppa and George
need is a special story to
help them fall asleep!

It is bedtime, but Peppa is not sleepy.
"Can you tell us a story, Daddy?"
"Of course," says Daddy Pig.
"As long as you promise to
go to sleep straight after."
"We promise!" cries Peppa.

"Once upon a time, in a castle,"
begins Daddy Pig, "there lived a little
princess called the Sleepy Princess."
"Was the Sleepy Princess pretty?"
asks Peppa.
"Yes," replies Daddy Pig. "She loved
looking at herself in the mirror all
day long."

Who else was living in the castle?" asks Peppa.

"Er, well . . ." says Daddy Pig.

"The others in the castle were . . . the Small Prince, Queen Mummy and King Daddy!" says Mummy Pig.

"That's right," says Daddy Pig.

"And there was a dragon at the castle," continues Daddy Pig.

"Dine-saw?" asks George.

"Oh yes, it wasn't a dragon – it was a dinosaur," says Daddy Pig.

"A huge fierce dinosaur! ROOAARRR!"

"Waaaahhh!" cries George.

Pig. "Maybe the dinosaur wasn't quite that fierce, Daddy Pig."

"Sorry, George," says Daddy Pig. "No, the dinosaur was very gentle. He ate lots of . . . grass."

"Daddy," says Peppa, "why was she called the Sleepy Princess?"

"I'm coming to that," says Daddy Pig. "You see, it was night time, the stars and moon were out and everyone got very, very sleepy . . . and the most sleepy of all was the Sleepy Princess."

Daddy Pig turned Peppa and George's light out.
"King Daddy carried the Sleepy Princess to bed in the castle tower, and she fell straight to sleep."
"Thank you for that story, King Daddy," whispers Mummy Pig.

"You're welcome, Queen Mummy," whispers Daddy Pig.
"It seems our little prince and princess enjoyed it, too!" adds Mummy Pig.
Peppa and George are fast asleep!
Snore! Snore! Snore!

Coach Ride

Prince George is pulling Princess Peppa along in her carriage. Can you spot six differences between the two pictures?

Colour in a crown as you spot each difference.

Answers: 1. Peppa has lost her crown. 2. The horse has a boot. 3. George's helmet has changed colour. 4. The carriage is floating in the air. 5. The horse's tail has changed colour. 6. The carriage wheel has changed colour.